A Time to Talk
Poems of Friendship

A
TIME
TO
TALK

Poems of Friendship

SELECTED BY

Myra Cohn Livingston

MARGARET K. McELDERRY BOOKS
New York

Maxwell Macmillan Canada • Toronto
Maxwell Macmillan International
New York   Oxford   Singapore   Sydney

For MAUREEN HAYES

Margaret K. McElderry Books
Macmillan Publishing Company
866 Third Avenue, New York, NY 10022

Maxwell Macmillan Canada, Inc.
1200 Eglinton Avenue East, Suite 200
Don Mills, Ontario M3C 3N1

Macmillan Publishing Company is part of the
Maxwell Communication Group of Companies.

First edition   Printed in the United States of America

Book design by Mina Greenstein
10 9 8 7 6 5 4 3 2 1

Library of Congress Cataloging-in-Publication Data
A time to talk : poems of friendship / selected by Myra Cohn
Livingston. — 1st ed.   p.   cm.
Summary: A collection of poems about friendship, by poets ranging
from ancient China to the present.
ISBN 0-689-50558-2
1. Friendship—Juvenile poetry. 2. Children's poetry. [1. Friendship—
Poetry. 2. Poetry—Collections.] I. Livingston, Myra Cohn.
PN6110.F8T56 1992 808.81'9353—dc20   91-42234

Acknowledgments

The editor and publisher thank the following for permission to reprint the copyrighted material listed below. Every effort has been made to locate all persons having any rights or interests in the material published here. Any existing rights not here acknowledged will, if the editor or publisher is notified, be duly acknowledged in future editions of this book.

JOAN AIKEN for "John's Song," from *The Skin Spinners*, copyright © 1976, Viking Penguin.

BOA EDITIONS, LTD., for "Lines for a Friend Who Left" by John Logan, copyright © 1989, from *John Logan: The Collected Poems* by John Logan. Reprinted with permission of BOA Editions, Ltd., 92 Park Ave., Brockport, NY 14420.

JOHN MALCOLM BRINNIN for "Nuns at Eve," from *The Sorrows of Cold Stone*, copyright © 1952, Dodd Mead.

GWENDOLYN BROOKS for "We Real Cool," from *Blacks*, copyright © 1987.

CARCANET PRESS LIMITED for "Trio" by Edwin Morgan, from *Collected Poems* by Edwin Morgan, copyright © 1982.

DEVIN-ADAIR, PUBLISHERS, INC., for "Monkeys" by Padraic Colum, from *Collected Poems*. Copyright © 1953 by Devin-Adair, Publishers, Inc., Old Greenwich, CT 06870. All rights reserved.

FABER AND FABER LIMITED PUBLISHERS for "A Revel" by Donagh MacDonagh, from *A Hungry Grass* by Donagh MacDonagh.

FARRAR, STRAUS & GIROUX, INC., for "And Yet the Earth Remains Unchanged" and "Friendship," from *In the Trail of the Wind* edited by John Bierhorst. Copyright © 1971 by John Bierhorst. Reprinted by permission of Farrar, Straus & Giroux, Inc.

MICHAEL GIBSON for "The Messages" by W. W. Gibson.

HARCOURT BRACE JOVANOVICH, INC., for "Accomplished Facts," from *Smoke and Steel* by Carl Sandburg, copyright © 1920 by Harcourt Brace Jovanovich, Inc., and renewed 1948 by Carl Sandburg. Reprinted by permission of the publisher. "One Parting," from *Honey and Salt*,

Contents

ONE

Friends

A Time to Talk

When a friend calls to me from the road
And slows his horse to a meaning walk,
I don't stand still and look around
On all the hills I haven't hoed,
And shout from where I am, "What is it?"
No, not as there is a time to talk.
I thrust my hoe in the mellow ground,
Blade-end up and five feet tall,
And plod: I go up to the stone wall
For a friendly visit.

Robert Frost

2

From Conversation at Tea

4

Yesterday I saw you
And you did not speak,
You walked as if—allow
Me to be trite—
You walked in a daze.
Do you concentrate
On things so bleak
You cannot see, for thought, your friends?
I know you saw my face
And yet as if our hands
Had never touched, you
Did not know me,
Or even seem to know
Yourself. This struck me strangely,
Your silence, since
Here we are sipping tea
And talking in present tense.
Let's agree, now we are together,
Friendship is forever.

Galway Kinnell

Raymond

Hair the color of pencil shavings,
eyes as dark as a night river,
best friend
since fifth grade
when he seemed to stop
growing.

Large enough
to blacken Danny Webb's eye
when he said,
"Hiya, pipsqueak,"
the first day of eighth grade,

small enough
to get into the movies as a kid.

At the Top Hat Café,
gave me one play
on his juke box quarters.

For three nights,
trusted me
with the false teeth
(uppers only)
he found
on a park bench.

In The Tattoo Emporium
let me help him
pick out the
eagle-holding-thunderbolt
he'd claim for his chest
the day he turned eighteen.

Paul B. Janeczko

From Accomplished Facts

Every year Emily Dickinson sent one friend
the first arbutus in her garden.

In a last will and testament Andrew Jackson
remembered a friend with the gift of George
Washington's pocket spy-glass.

Napoleon too, in a last testament, mentioned a silver
watch taken from the bedroom of Frederick the Great,
and passed along this trophy to a particular friend.

O. Henry took a blood carnation from his coat lapel
and handed it to a country girl starting work in a
bean bazaar, and scribbled: "Peach blossoms may or
may not stay pink in city dust."

So it goes. Some things we buy, some not . . .

Carl Sandburg

The Arroyo, Sergio, and Me

We went in that arroyo just to cuss
down everything and everyone to mud
at least a hundred times and maybe worse
because we could, just that, because we could

and no one ever said a thing to us,
not even when we screamed for teacher blood
those summer afternoons of *go to hell*,
of maim and rape and Claudia and kill.

So boy! was that one heck of a you bet! place,
and what we found there, me and him, was swell,
the swellest, underneath that rotting brace
of railroad bridge: a rounded, solid, dull

and beautiful steel ball the Southern P.,
who'd blow their whistle if they saw you call,
had used for ballast maybe, or bombs—
what do caboose men do when they get bored?

We buried it, cause it was perfect; it
was all we talked about, till we forgot.

Alberto Ríos

On the Yo-yang Tower with His Friend, Chia

Here from this tower we may view
The whole fair region of Yo-yang,
And the winding river
Opening into the Tung-ting Lake.

O wild geese, flying past,
Take away with you the sorrow of the heart!
And, come, thou mountain, give us thy happy moon!

Here will we sit to feast
And tarry a while with the clouds
And pass the cup high above the world of cares.

When we are goodly warm with wine,
Then, thou cooling breeze, arise!
Come and blow as we dance!
And our sleeves will flap like wings.

Li Po

*translated from the Chinese
by Shigeyoshi Obata*

The Refusal to Be Wrecked

I have
planted a trusted anchor
into your choppy sea
no matter how waves will waver
the stock
the shank
the arm
no matter
how cold
the water
the fluke
the crown
the chain
no matter
how much
I shiver
the throat
the bill
the ring

Avast! the storms will all be weathered *Belay!*
the boat will hold together

Lillian Morrison

The Departure

When you go away
you become everything I believe
you are, the steady light
from the lamps, warm
from a distance on my skin,
the piano still playing
somewhere in my mind, curtains
blowing at the window
speaking to me.

Frank Steele

At Long Last

I saw you walking
On Fifth Avenue,
Threading thru the crowd,
Aloof. Head held unusually high for a native
An ocean away,
Thinking perhaps of
Those balmy days
In Gabon.
At first you rebuffed
My glances, in favor of the fairer races.
But now I could go and throw
My arms around you
On Fifth Avenue,
Oblivious to the roar of the
Crowd. We, two, alone.
I in my red velvet dashiki
That everyone says looks
So good on me,
And you in your tan corduroy
Gayla that makes you stand out
Even in a festive crowd.

Lindsay Patterson

a total stranger one black day
knocked living the hell out of me—

who found forgiveness hard because
my(as it happened)self he was

—but now that fiend and i are such
immortal friends the other's each

e. e. cummings

Silence

'Tis better to sit here beside the sea,
  Here on the spray-kissed beach,
In silence, that between such friends as we
  Is full of deepest speech.

Paul Laurence Dunbar

Noises

*The eternal silence of these
Infinite spaces
frightens me.*
—Pascal

I want to write a poem
                for you
that will sound
                feel like the little electric tingles
skittering over my skin when I think your name
I want to tug
                pull your face to smiles
                                when you read the words

I want to write a poem
                that will shimmer
and stand against your mind like yesterdays
I want to make visions
that will rage through your dreams
I want miles and miles of me
                                living inside you
racing with your blood
                a poem of you coming
jumping into my life
                your eyes calm
and your voice
                like a vanishing summer storm
rolling around in me.

I want to find noisy things
                to fill the void

I want to jam the silence
                    of these spaces
with our whispers   our laughter
I want to fill the emptiness with our eye
                              mind contact
I want the feeling to slide between us in waves
smothering distance
                  stifling fears
                            exploding the vacuum
tall sounds
          of people living
small sounds
            feathering
                  billowing vibrating
connecting   youtometoyoutometo
                        you to me
                              to you.

Fred Johnson

■

Kyrnos, be flexible in character, always adapting
      your own mood to that of the friend you chance to be
           with;
be as the lithe and tentacled octopus, altering color
      so that it matches and loses itself in the rock where it
           clings;
so be you; be now, like this, then change your complexion;
      better you should be subtle than stubbornly always the
           same.

Theógnis of Mégara

translated from the Greek
by Richmond Lattimore

The Telephone

"When I was just as far as I could walk
From here today,
There was an hour
All still
When leaning with my head against a flower
I heard you talk.
Don't say I didn't, for I heard you say—
You spoke from that flower on the window sill—
Do you remember what it was you said?"

"First tell me what it was you thought you heard."

"Having found the flower and driven a bee away,
I leaned my head,
And holding by the stalk,
I listened and I thought I caught the word—
What was it? Did you call me by my name?
Or did you say—
Someone said 'Come'—I heard it as I bowed."

"I may have thought as much, but not aloud."

"Well, so I came."

Robert Frost

The Conspiracy

You send me your poems,
I'll send you mine.

Things tend to awaken
even through random communication.

Let us suddenly
proclaim spring. And jeer

at the others,
all the others.

I will send a picture too
if you will send me one of you.

Robert Creeley

The Song Turning Back into Itself 2

A Song for Little Children

Always it's either
a beginning
or some end:
the baby's being born
or its parents are
dying, fading on
like the rose
of the poem
withers, its light going out
while gardens come in
to bloom

Let us stand on streetcorners
in the desolate era
& propose a new kind
of crazyness

Let us salute one another
one by one
two by two
the soft belly
moving towards
the long sideburns
the adams apple
or no apple at all

Let there be
in this crazyness
a moon
a violin
a drum

Let the beautiful brown girl
join hands with
her black sister
her golden sister
her milkskinned sister
their eternal wombs
turning with the moon

Let there be a flute
to squeal above
the beat & the bowing
to open us up
that the greens
the blues
the yellows
the reds
the silvers &
indescribable rusts
might flow out
amazingly
& blend
with the wind

Let the wobbly spin
of the earth
be a delight
wherein
a caress forms
the most perfect circle

Let the always be love
the beginning be love
love the only
possible
end

Al Young

Friendship

Like a quetzal plume, a fragrant flower,
friendship sparkles:
like heron plumes, it weaves itself into finery.
Our song is a bird calling out like a jingle:
how beautiful you make it sound!
Here, among flowers that enclose us,
among flowery boughs you are singing.

Anonymous

*translated from the Aztec
by John Bierhorst*

From Praise Songs
for Various
Chiefs and Sultans

May God preserve you in the same way,
As He does not allow friendship to grow old: . . .

J. R. Patterson

T W O

Friends in Company

And Yet the Earth Remains Unchanged

Ah, flowers that we wear!
Ah, songs that we raise!
—we are on our way to the Realm of Mystery!
If only for one day,
let us be together, my friends!
We must leave our flowers behind us,
we must leave our songs:
and yet the earth remains unchanged.
My friends, enjoy! Friends! Enjoy!

Anonymous

*translated from the Aztec
by John Bierhorst*

We Real Cool

The Pool Players
Seven at the Golden Shovel

We real cool. We
Left school. We

Lurk late. We
Strike straight. We

Sing sin. We
Thin gin. We

Jazz June. We
Die soon.

Gwendolyn Brooks

Wine

Spring wine . . . autumn wine, give me
my comrades, a table upon which fall
equinoctial leaves, and let the great river of the world
turn a little pale in the stir of its sound
far from our songs.
                    I am a good companion.

   You didn't come into this house so I might tear off
   a piece of your life. Perhaps when you leave
   you'll take something of mine: chestnuts, roses or
   a surety of roots or boats
   that I wanted to share with you, comrade.

   Sing with me until the glasses
   spill over leaving purple remains
   on the table
                    This honey comes to your mouth
   from out of the earth, from its sunken clusters.

How many are missing, shadows of song,
                                        comrades
I loved face to face, distilling from my life
the peerless virile science I profess,
friendship, grove of rugged tenderness.

Give me your hand, meet with me,
simply, don't look for anything in my words
beyond the emanation of a bare plant.

Why ask more from me than from a workman? You
   already know
that I forged my interred smithery stroke by stroke
and that I do not care to speak except as is my speech.
Go out and look for doctors if you don't like the wind.

We'll sing along with the sharp wine
of the earth: we'll knock back the glasses of autumn,
and the guitar or the silence will go on bringing
love-lines, the language of non-existent rivers,
well-beloved stanzas with no sense at all.

Pablo Neruda

*translated from the Spanish
by Anthony Kerrigan*

Hares and Hounds

In autumn, chained to classrooms, we still can hear
The call of the sea. When the week is done,
We break our fetters
And down to the shore we go with scarves and sweaters,
Down to the shore, where the wind is sapping
The strength of the aged sun.
We're ready, with shouting and leaping and side-slapping
To play some boisterous game and run.

"Jane, what shall it be?"
Said Penelope, Anne and Helen, turning to me.
But they'd wait for no answer. "Hares and Hounds!"
Cried Helen, with the longest legs—she's tallest.
"We'll be hares. You two can chase!"
(That's me and Andrew—he's the smallest),
And over the windy sands with leaps and bounds
Away they race.
So, while the tide was mounting,
I helped Andrew with his counting,
Till, "Two hundred up!" he cried. "That way
They went!" He'd squinted,
And off toward Roman Dune we sprinted.

Long before East Head we lost the trace—
No twigs or markings, no scribbled arrows.
The beach soon narrows,
And the tide clawed up the space.
No sign but a sail
Like a waving handkerchief, far out;

No sound but the muffled shout
Of sea and shingle, and the wail
Of gulls crying, "Here!
                    here!
                            here!"

But where?
The sea had wiped out the trail,
And the rising gull-tossing gale
Was whipping the foam from the waves like froth from ale.

Then back with dragging steps we went,
Bad-tempered, tired and spent;
We were hounds no more, just fools and mutts.
And suddenly Andrew said, "I know where they are!"
And pulled me through the hedge, behind the huts . . .

Those lazy hares had *not* gone far.
Those cosy-crazy hares,
Those "wind's-too-cold-for-us-these-days"-y hares
Were huddled
                reading comics
                            in the car.

Ian Serraillier

Nuns at Eve

On St. Martin's evening green
Imaginary diamond, between
The vestry buttress and the convent wall,
Solemn as sea birds in a sanctuary,
Under the statue of the Virgin they play baseball.
They are all named Mary,
Sister Mary, Mary Anthony or Mary Rose,
And when the softball flies
In the shadow of the cross
The little chaplet of the Virgin's hands
Contains their soft excitements like a house.

A flying habit traces
The unprecedented rounding of the bases
By Sister Mary Agatha, who thanks God
For the easy triple and turns her eyes toward home;
As *Mary, Mother, help me* echoes in her head,
Mild cries from the proud team
Encourage her, and the obliging sun,
Dazzling the pitcher's box
With a last celestial light upon
The gold-spiked halo of the Virgin in her niche,
Leads Sister Mary John to a wild pitch.

Prayer wins the game.
As Sister Mary Agatha comes sailing home
Through infield dusk, like birds fanwise
In the vague cloisters of slow-rising mist,
Winners and losers gather in to praise
The fleetness of a bride of Christ.
Flushed and humble, Agatha collects the bats

And balls, while at her belt
Catchers' and pitchers' mitts
—Brute fingers, toes and gross lopsided heads—
Fumble the ropes of her long swinging beads.

John Malcolm Brinnin

From **The Prelude**

Book II

> When summer came,
> Our pastime was, on bright half-holidays,
> To sweep along the plain of Windermere
> With rival oars; and the selected bourne
> Was now an Island musical with birds
> That sang and ceased not; now a Sister Isle
> Beneath the oaks' umbrageous covert, sown
> With lilies of the valley like a field;
> And now a third small Island, where survived
> In solitude the ruins of a shrine
> Once to Our Lady dedicate, and served
> Daily with chaunted rites. In such a race
> So ended, disappointment could be none,
> Uneasiness, or pain, or jealousy:
> We rested in the shade, all pleased alike,
> Conquered and conqueror . . .

William Wordsworth

Friends

Some of my best friends are white boys.
When I meet 'em
I treat 'em
Just the same as if
They was people.

Ray Durem

To His Friend
to Avoid Contention of Words

Words beget Anger: Anger brings forth blowes:
Blowes make of dearest friends immortall Foes.
For which prevention (Sociate) let there be
Betwixt us two no more *Logomachie.*
Farr better 'twere for either to be mute,
Then for to murder friendship, by dispute.

Robert Herrick

The Golden Palace

We go to the Golden Palace:
We set out the jade cups.
We summon the honoured guests
To enter at the Golden Gate.
They enter at the Golden Gate
And go to the Golden Hall.
In the Eastern Kitchen the meat is sliced and ready—
Roast beef and boiled pork and mutton.
The Master of the Feast hands round the wine.
The harp-players sound their clear chords.

The cups are pushed aside and we face each other
   at chess:
The rival pawns are marshalled rank against rank.
The fire glows and the smoke puffs and curls;
From the incense-burner rises a delicate fragrance.
The clear wine has made our cheeks red;
Round the table joy and peace prevail.
May those who shared in this day's delight
Through countless autumns enjoy like felicity.

Anonymous

*translated from the Chinese
by Arthur Waley*

From Assassination Poems

The Friends

They turn to each other quickly
weaving a basket, trying to weave
a basket of words
watertight, greased to hold grief

John Ridland

To Lou Gehrig

We've been to the wars together;
We took our foes as they came;
And always you were the leader,
And ever you played the game.

Idol of cheering millions,
  Records are yours by sheaves;
Iron of frame they hailed you,
  Decked you with laurel leaves.
But higher than that we hold you,
  We who have known you best,
Knowing the way you came through
  Every human test.

Let this be a silent token
Of lasting friendship's gleam
And all that we've left unspoken—
Your pals of the Yankee team.

                    John Kieran

Old Friends

Oh, sure am I when come to die,
And through Death's portals go,
Those cats, and dogs, and little white mice,
And birds, I used to know,
Shall all come rushing to welcome me,
Their friend of the long ago.

And the cats will purr, "We've missed you, sir,
And we know you missed us too."
And the dogs will bark, "Good morning, friend,
We've waited long for you."
And the little white mice shall squeak with joy,
And the birds will chirp and coo.

And happen what may on the Judgement Day,
I shall not affrighted be,
If the cats and dogs, and all weak dumb things
That on earth were dear to see,
Should receive from God the gift of speech,
For I know that they'll plead for me.

A. Muir

Trio

Coming up Buchanan Street, quickly, on a sharp winter
    evening
a young man and two girls, under the Christmas lights—
The young man carries a new guitar in his arms,
the girl on the inside carries a very young baby,
and the girl on the outside carries a chihuahua.
And the three of them are laughing, their breath rises
in a cloud of happiness, and as they pass
the boy says, "Wait till he sees this but!"
The chihuahua has a tiny Royal Stewart tartan coat like a
    teapot-holder,
the baby in its white shawl is all bright eyes and mouth like
    favours in a fresh sweet cake,
the guitar swells out under its milky plastic cover, tied at
    the neck with silver tinsel tape and a brisk sprig of
    mistletoe.
Orphean sprig! Melting baby! Warm chihuahua!
The vale of tears is powerless before you.
Whether Christ is born, or is not born, you
put paid to fate, it abdicates
                              under the Christmas lights.

Monsters of the year
go blank, are scattered back,
can't bear this march of three.

41

—And the three have passed, vanished in the crowd
(yet not vanished, for in their arms they wind
the life of men and beasts, and music,
laughter ringing them round like a guard)
at the end of this winter's day.

Edwin Morgan

A Revel

I'd fill up the house with guests this minute
And have them drinking in every room
And the laughter wrecking the garden quiet.
Citymen dressed in a sober style
Who never soiled a buckled shoe,
And wild country boys with a frieze coat flapping
That were never within an ass's roar
Of a city street, and shining girls
In every fashion. I'd call them in
Out of every year for the past ten hundred
And make them safe at their own table,
The men whose blood is safe in my veins.

I'd have no aged ghosts struggling out of the grave,
But lively lads that I'd borrow from time,
And till Peter's bird set them screaming homeward
The neighbours hearing that heady laughter
Would think it a wedding or a wake.

I'd leave uncertain the hour of departure,
But while night was pasted black on the windows
We'd talk of love, and blood to blood
We'd speak one language; tinker and poet,
The tramps who were hurled from their own possessions
And the wealthy men would talk flesh to flesh,
The years dissolved that were huge between them.

And one would tell of the time of hunger,
The mouths stained green in a ditch's end,
Earth cleared for action and hunger rearing
High in the belly, a country withered

Before Spring's rally. But another would shout
Of a night of drinking, and senses loosed
And the traces broken
And the drink as mild as the milky way.

Fathers would lean on their grandsons' shoulders
And great-great-grandsons pass a glass
And laugh in the face of their great-grandfather;
And together we'd find the spirit within us
Too wild to be bound by house or wall,
And only the dawn and the cock's alarm
Could save the town. Then home they'd rush
Hot in their leather.

Heir to them all
I'd count them over, recall the nose
And the curve of the mouth, till sleep would slip
Through the wakening window and curl about me,
And I, like them, would be lost in time.

Donagh MacDonagh

THREE

Strange Friends, False Friends

Useless Words

So long as we speak the same language and never understand
    each other,
So long as the spirals of our words snarl and interlock
And clutch each other with the irreckonable gutturals,
Well . . .

Carl Sandburg

If I Should Die Tonight

If I should die tonight
And you should come to my cold
    corpse and say,
Weeping and heartsick o'er my life-
    less clay—
If I should die tonight,
And you should come in deepest
    grief and woe—
And say: "Here's that ten dollars
    that I owe,"
    I might arise in my large white
        cravat
    And say, "What's that?"

If I should die tonight
And you should come to my cold
    corpse and kneel,
Clasping my bier to show the grief
    you feel,
I say, if I should die tonight
And you should come to me, and
    there and then
Just even hint 'bout paying me that
    ten,
    I might arise the while,
    But I'd drop dead again.

Ben King

From As You Like It

Act II, Scene 7

Blow, blow, thou winter wind,
Thou art not so unkind
    As man's ingratitude;
Thy tooth is not so keen
Because thou art not seen,
    Although thy breath be rude.
Heigh-ho! sing, heigh-ho! unto the green holly:
Most friendship is feigning, most loving mere folly:
    Then, heigh-ho, the holly!
        This life is most jolly.

Freeze, freeze, thou bitter sky,
That dost not bite so nigh
    As benefits forgot:
Though thou the waters warp,
Thy sting is not so sharp
    As friend remember'd not.
Heigh-ho! sing, heigh-ho! unto the green holly:
Most friendship is feigning, most loving mere folly:
    Then, heigh-ho, the holly!
        This life is most jolly.

William Shakespeare

From Japanese Beetles

3 *To Someone Who Insisted I Look Up Someone*

I rang them up while touring Timbuctoo,
Those bosom chums to whom you're known as *Who?*

X. J. Kennedy

Deirdre

Do not let any woman read this verse;
It is for men, and after them their sons
And their son's sons.

The time comes when our hearts sink utterly;
When we remember Deirdre and her tale,
And that her lips are dust.

Once she did tread the earth: men took her hand;
They looked into her eyes and said their say,
And she replied to them.

More than a thousand years it is since she
Was beautiful: she trod the grass;
She saw the clouds.

A thousand years! The grass is still the same,
The clouds as lovely as they were that time
When Deirdre was alive.

But there has never been a woman born
Who was so beautiful, not one so beautiful
Of all the women born.

Let all men go apart and mourn together;
No man can love her; not a man
Can ever be her lover.

No man can bend before her: no man say—
What could one say to her? There are no words
That one could say to her!

Now she is but a story that is told
Beside the fire! No man can ever be
The friend of that poor queen.

James Stephens

The Maze

When I tried
to track the pathways
of your brain

I got lost.
Up, down, sideways
I no longer knew

where I was
what with the vistas
the electric shocks

and then I kept wanting
to go two ways
at once.

Lillian Morrison

A Friend

Who borrows all your ready cash,
And with it cuts a mighty dash,
Proving the lender weak and rash?—
                              Your friend!

Who finds out every secret fault,
Misjudges every word and thought,
And makes you pass for worse than nought?—
                              Your friend!

Who wins your money at deep play,
Then tells you that the world doth say,
" 'Twere wise from clubs you kept away"?—
                              Your friend!

Who sells you, for the longest price,
Horses, a dealer, in a trice,
Would find unsound and full of vice?—
                              Your friend!

Who eats your dinners, then looks shrewd;
Wishes you had a cook like Ude,
For then much oftener would intrude?—
                              Your friend!

Who tells you that you've shocking wine,
And owns that, though he sports not fine,
Crockford's the only place to dine?—
                              Your friend!

Who wheedles you with words most fond
To sign for him a heavy bond,
"Or else, by Jove, must quick abscond"?—
                                    Your friend!

Who makes you all the interest pay,
With principal, some future day,
And laughs at what you then may say?—
                                    Your friend!

Who makes deep love unto your wife,
Knowing you prize her more than life,
And breeds between you hate and strife?—
                                    Your friend!

Who, when you've got into a brawl,
Insists that out your man you call,
Then gets you shot, which ends it all?—
                                    Your friend!

Marguerite Power

The Ball and the Club

I shot a golf ball into the air;
It fell toward earth, I knew not where;
For who hath eye so strong and keen,
As to follow the flight of my ball to the green.

I lost a club I could not spare,
And searched for it most everywhere;
For who hath sight so keen and quick
As to trace the course of a missing stick.

Long, long afterwards, in an oak,
I found the golf ball still unbroke;
And the club—with a couple of nicks and a bend,
I found again in the bag of a friend.

Forbes Lindsay

We talked as Girls do—
Fond, and late—
We speculated fair, on every subject, but the Grave—
Of ours, none affair—

We handled Destinies, as cool—
As we—Disposers—be—
And God, a Quiet Party
To our Authority—

But fondest, dwelt upon Ourself
As we eventual—be—
When Girls to Women, softly raised
We—occupy—Degree—

We parted with a contract
To cherish, and to write
But Heaven made both, impossible
Before another night.

Emily Dickinson

From Cantares

II

I lied—trusting you knew
I could not lie to you.

Beloved friend, I lied, and am forgiven: but I
Cannot forgive that you believed my lie!

Leonora Speyer

From Conversation at Tea

5

I have struck gems in several friends,
Perhaps in more than most, certainly
In more than you, whose delicate tea
Tends more to water. But this is surely
Because the stars rule our destiny
Or God plots out our ends.

My drink is crude and bitter
But at least I made the stuff myself.
You might concede that nature made me better
At hunting diamond mines than you, yet if
You doubt, let me recount the story of
Two friendships now a-tatter.

Chris was one, whose fine fierce spirit spent
Its up-pent fury arguing with me
Who wandered worlds with him. One day he penned
His testament and died. If he could see
Me now, against my heart's depravity,
He could not lift, for tears, his hand.

Another friend was Gib, who did not die,
But wished to change the world, and found
It would not change. His heart fell utterly
To dust, though sometimes still he smiles around
The corners of his mouth. I saw him ruined,
He cannot therefore speak to me.

These friends were fast, for life-long working,
But as you see, a friend is not eternal.
Sometimes walking on the streets, or talking
Over tea, I drowse, conversing with an angel
Of all those days when friends went well,
And see no half-friends lurking.

Galway Kinnell

The Bath

Broad is the Gate and wide the Path
That leads man to his daily bath;
But ere you spend the shining hour
With plunge and spray, with sluice and show'r—

With all that teaches you to dread
The bath as little as your bed—
Remember, whereso'er you be,
To shut the door and turn the key!

I had a friend—my friend no more!—
Who failed to bolt the bath-room door;

A maiden-aunt of his, one day,
Walked in, as half-submerged he lay!

But did not notice nephew John
And turned the boiling water on!

He had no time, or even scope,
To camouflage himself with soap,
But gave a yell and flung aside
The sponge, 'neath which he sought to hide!

It fell to earth, I know not where!
He beat his breast in his despair,
And then, like Venus from the foam,
Sprang into view, and made for home!

His aunt fell fainting to the ground!
Alas! They never brought her round!

She died, intestate, in her prime,
The victim of another's crime;

And John can never quite forget
How, by a breach of etiquette,
He lost, at one fell swoop (or plunge)
His aunt, his honour, and his sponge!

Harry Graham

My friend attacks my friend
Oh Battle picturesque!
Then I turn Soldier too,
And he turns Satirist!
How martial is this place!
Had I a mighty gun
I think I'd shoot the human race
And then to glory run!

Emily Dickinson

Song

To become a chief's favorite
Is not always comfortable;
It is like making friends
With a hippopotamus.

Hugh Tracey

Anthony

Your absent name at rollcall was more present
than you ever were, forever
on parole in the back of the class.
The first morning you were gone,
we practiced penmanship to keep our minds
off you. My first
uncoiled chains of connecting circles,
oscilloscopic hills;
my carved-up desk, rippled as a washboard.

A train cut you in half in the Jersey marshes.
You played there after school.
I thought of you and felt afraid.
One awkward *a* multiplied into a fence
running across the page.
I copied out two rows of *b*'s.
The caboose of the last *d* ran smack against
the margin. Nobody even liked you!
My *e*'s and *f*'s travelled over the snowy landscape
on parallel tracks—the blue guidelines
that kept our letters even.

The magician sawed his wife in half.
He passed his hand through the gulf of air
where her waist should be.
Divided into two boxes, she turned and smiled
and all her ten toes flexed.
I skipped a line.
I dotted the disconnected body of each *i*
At the bottom of the page,
I wrote your name. Erased it.
Wrote it, and erased again.

Jane Shore

'Tis true—They shut me in the Cold—
But then—Themselves were warm
And could not know the feeling 'twas—
Forget it—Lord—of Them—

Let not my Witness hinder Them
In Heavenly esteem—
No Paradise could be—Conferred
Through Their beloved Blame—

The Harm They did—was short—And since
Myself—who bore it—do—
Forgive Them—Even as Myself—
Or else—forgive not me—

Emily Dickinson

And now, kind friends, what I have wrote,
  I hope you will pass o'er,
And not criticize as some have done
  Hitherto herebefore.

Julia Moore

FOUR

Lost Friends

From Chorus from *Medea*

I have seen it with my own eyes,
I have heard my own heart tell me:
There is no city, no,
No friend who will give you pity
In the hour of your deepest woe.
O, let him perish in darkness
Who is faithless to his friends
And lets his heart stay frozen!
Let no such man be my friend!

Euripides

translated from the Greek
by Frederic Prokosch

Adrian Henri's Talking
After Christmas Blues

Well I woke up this mornin' it was Christmas Day
And the birds were singing the night away
I saw my stocking lying on the chair
Looked right to the bottom but you weren't there
there was

> apples
> > oranges
> > > chocolates
> > > > . . . . aftershave

—but no you.

So I went downstairs and the dinner was fine
There was pudding and turkey and lots of wine
And I pulled those crackers with a laughing face
Till I saw there was no one in your place
there was

> mincepies
> > brandy
> > > nuts and raisins
> > > > . . . . mashed potato

—but no you.

Now it's New Year and it's Auld Lang Syne
And it's 12 o'clock and I'm feeling fine
Should Auld Acquaintance be Forgot?

I don't know girl, but it hurts a lot
there was

       whisky
       vodka
          dry Martini (stirred
             but not shaken)
. . . . and 12 New Year resolutions
—all of them about you.

So it's all the best for the year ahead
As I stagger upstairs and into bed
Then I looked at the pillow by my side
. . . . I tell you baby I almost cried
there'll be

       Autumn
       Summer
        Spring
          . . . . and Winter
—all of them without you.

Adrian Henri

From **The Thousand and Second Night**

3. Carnivals

Three good friends in as many months have complained,
"You were nice, James, before your trip. Or so
I thought. But you have changed. I know, I know,
People do change. Well, I'm surprised, I'm pained."

Before they disappeared into the night
Of what they said, I'd make a stab at mouthing
Promises that meant precisely nothing
And never saved my face. For they were right . . .

James Merrill

Monkeys

Two little creatures
With faces the size of
A pair of pennies
Are clasping each other.
"Ah, do not leave me,"
One says to the other,
In the high monkey-
Cage in the beast-shop.

There are no people to gape at them now,
For people are loth to
Peer in the dimness;
Have they not builded
Streets and playhouses,
Sky-signs and bars,
To lose the loneliness
Shaking the hearts
Of the two little Monkeys?

Yes. But who watches
The penny-small faces
Can hear the voices:
"Ah, do not leave me;
Suck I will give you,
Warmth and clasping,
And if you slip from
This beam I can never
Find you again."

Dim is the evening
And chill is the weather;
There, drawn from their colored
Hemisphere,
The apes lilliputian
With faces the size of
A pair of pennies,
And voices as low as
The flow of my blood.

Padraic Colum

Lines for a Friend Who Left

*"Ich starre, wie des Steins Inneres starrat."**
—R. M. Rilke

Something vague waxes or wanes.
I have been grieving since you've gone,
and I am stark as the heart of the stone.
I have this grief because you are a ghost
and a thief. Since you left I have missed
my own self. For your absence
steals my presence.
Next I lost my dignity. At night
I put on the dirty shirt
and coat you left
and go out
to hunt for you in the bar or street
feeling your private warmth. Last night
I thought I saw your very face
(voice of another)
in the place of a folk singer.
(The heavy mouth almost seemed to sneer
at the end. I could not be sure.)
I have not heard
since you've gone, so I still yearn
for any sign
of your life. For if you died
I did too. I
Can no longer quite
make out your body's breadth and height,

* "I stare, like a stone stares."

76

and there is something vague that grows in me
like a dead child.
Write
or come back, before I forget
what we both look like.

John Logan

Two Years Later

Has no one said those daring
Kind eyes should be more learn'd?
Or warned you how despairing
The moths are when they are burned?
I could have warned you; but you are young,
So we speak a different tongue.

O you will take whatever's offered
And dream that all the world's a friend,
Suffer as your mother suffered,
Be as broken in the end.
But I am old and you are young,
And I speak a barbarous tongue.

William Butler Yeats

let it go—the
smashed word broken
open vow or
the oath cracked length
wise—let it go it
was sworn to
                go

let them go—the
truthful liars and
the false fair friends
and the boths and
neithers—you must let them go they
were born
                to go

let all go—the
big small middling
tall bigger really
the biggest and all
things—let all go
dear
        so comes love

                    e. e. cummings

That she forgot me was the least
I felt it second pain
That I was worthy to forget
Was most I thought upon.

Faithful was all that I could boast
But Constancy became
To her, by her innominate,
A something like a shame.

Emily Dickinson

Carl Perusick

Tonight I think of him, my kind unaggressive friend
who gestured to me like a man caught in the rain,
sitting on the rocks along the river.
I remember the fog glistening in the faded light
and the bewildered houses
walking into the river on their skinny wooden legs
while we hauled logs out of the water.
When I cut my foot on a piece of glass,
he carried me home on his back
and I remember, too, our reflection in the store windows
looked like a large upright turtle.
We had built a raft from driftwood
and that night we almost made it across.

Anthony Petrosky

Tomorrow

Your best friend is gone,
your other friend, too.
Now the dream that used to turn in your sleep,
sails into the year's coldest night.

What did you say?
Or was it something you did?
It makes no difference—the house of breath collapsing
around your voice, your voice burning, are nothing to
    worry about.

Tomorrow your friends will come back;
your moist open mouth will bloom in the glass of
    storefronts.
Yes. Yes. Tomorrow they will come back and you
will invent an ending that comes out right.

Mark Strand

One Parting

Why did he write to her,
"I can't live with you"?
And why did she write to him,
"I can't live without you"?
For he went west, she went east,
And they both lived.

Carl Sandburg

From **Christabel**

Alas! they had been friends in youth;
But whispering tongues can poison truth;
And constancy lives in realms above;
And life is thorny; and youth is vain;
And to be wroth with one we love
Doth work like madness in the brain.

They parted—ne'er to meet again!
But never either found another
To free the hollow heart from paining—
They stood aloof, the scars remaining,
Like cliffs which had been rent asunder;
A dreary sea now flows between.
But neither heat, nor frost, nor thunder,
Shall wholly do away, I ween,
The marks of that which once hath been.

Samuel Taylor Coleridge

The Swamp

I saw many friends, and among them the friend I loved most
Helplessly sink into the swamp
I pass by daily.

And a drowning was not over
In a single morning. Often it took
Weeks; this made it more terrible.
And the memory of our long talks together
About the swamp, that already
Had claimed so many.

Helpless I watched him, leaning back
Covered with leeches
In the shimmering
Softly moving slime:
Upon the sinking face
The ghastly
Blissful smile.

Bertolt Brecht

*translated from the German
by Naomi Replansky*

Coming Again to Heng-yang, I Mourn for Liu Tsung-yuan

I remember a former day when I and a friend
Said farewell on the bank of the River Hsiang.
In the sunlit woods, my horse neighed;
Into a curve of the hills his sail vanished.
My horse's neigh follows the old road,
The sail vanishes like a flash of lightning.
Spring comes to a thousand leagues of water weeds,
But now my old friend cannot be found.

Liu Yü-hsi

*translated from the Chinese
by Daniel Bryant*

FIVE

Friends
Remembered

Poem

I loved my friend.
He went away from me.
There's nothing more to say.
The poem ends,
Soft as it began—
I loved my friend.

Langston Hughes

Composed on Horseback, Returning from Lakeview Pavilion at Hangchow, Presented to Yu-ju and Lo-tao

River's glint and mountain mist were floating in green;
At sunset we made to return, they stayed a little longer.
Hereafter this scene shall always enter into my dreams;
In dreams I can wander with my old friends.

Wang An-shih

*translated from the Chinese
by Jan W. Walls*

How will you manage
To cross alone
The autumn mountain
Which was so hard to get across
Even when we went the two of us together?

Princess Daihaku
translated from the Japanese

The Skimming Stone

in memory of Billy Knight,
who died of a heart attack, age 38

The factory on the river, during lunch
We'd skim stones to a current brown and slow.
The shore was pebbles that our boots would scrunch
As we searched back and forth for stones to throw.
Most of the stones were poor New England slate;
A few had—smooth and round—the proper weight,
And we'd spin off long runs and argue whether
To count concluding skips that merged together.

Once when the whistle called us from the shore,
You pocketed a stone. Was it for luck?
Or did you feel a specially close rapport
That day with life, with youth? Or were you struck
Merely that the stone's smooth warmth implied
A longer rather than a shorter ride?

Timothy Steele

The Corridor

It may have been the pride in me for aught
I know, or just a patronizing whim;
But call it freak or fancy, or what not,
I cannot hide that hungry face of him.

I keep a scant half-dozen words he said,
And every now and then I lose his name;
He may be living or he may be dead,
But I must have him with me all the same.

I knew it, and I knew it all along,—
And felt it once or twice, or thought I did;
But only as a glad man feels a song
That sounds around a stranger's coffin lid.

I knew it, and he knew it, I believe,
But silence held us alien to the end;
And I have now no magic to retrieve
That year, to stop that hunger for a friend.

Edwin Arlington Robinson

Remember

Remember me when I am gone away,
  Gone far away into the silent land;
  When you can no more hold me by the hand,
Nor I half turn to go yet turning stay.
Remember me when no more day by day
  You tell me of our future that you planned:
  Only remember me; you understand
It will be late to counsel then or pray.

Yet if you should forget me for a while
  And afterwards remember, do not grieve:
  For if the darkness and corruption leave
  A vestige of the thoughts that once I had,
Better by far you should forget and smile
  Than that you should remember and be sad.

Christina Rossetti

The Messages

"I cannot quite remember . . . There were five
Dropt dead beside me in the trench—and three
Whispered their dying messages to me . . ."

Back from the trenches, more dead than alive,
Stone-deaf and dazed, and with a broken knee
He hobbled slowly, muttering vacantly:

"I cannot quite remember . . . There were five
Dropt dead beside me in the trench—and three
Whispered their dying messages to me . . .

"Their friends are waiting, wondering how they thrive—
Waiting a word in silence patiently . . .
But what they said, or who their friends may be

"I cannot quite remember . . . There were five
Dropt dead beside me in the trench—and three
Whispered their dying messages to me . . ."

Wilfrid Wilson Gibson

Funebrial Reflections

Among the anthropophagi
People's friends are people's sarcophagi.

Ogden Nash

A Kind of Hero

At school he was revered, yet lonely.
No other boy, however much
He might dream of it,
Dared to try to be his friend.
He walked, gaunt and piratical,
All bones and grin,
Towards his inescapable end.

Revered, but not by authority,
He poured ink into the new hat
Of the French master,
Painted the blackboard white,
Swore at the huge Principal,
Refused to bend
And invited him to a free fight.

In memory he is beautiful,
But only his desperate gold
Hair might have been so.
Vaguely we understood,
And were grateful, that he performed
Our lawless deeds;
Punished, he allowed us to be good.

The end: he was killed at Alamein.
He wore handcuffs on the troopship
Going out, his webbing
All scrubbed as white as rice;
And we, or others like us,
Were promoted
By his last derisive sacrifice.

Vernon Scannell

Paying Calls

I went by footpath and by stile
    Beyond where bustle ends,
Strayed here a mile and there a mile
    And called upon some friends.

On certain ones I had not seen
    For years past did I call,
And then on others who had been
    The oldest friends of all.

It was the time of midsummer
    When they had used to roam;
But now, though tempting was the air,
    I found them all at home.

I spoke to one and other of them
    By mound and stone and tree
Of things we had done ere days were dim
    But they spoke not to me.

Thomas Hardy

Holes

Strangest of gaps
their goneness—
mother, father, loved friends

the black holes
of the astronomer
are not more mysterious

this kind of hole
will not be filled
with candle flames
or even a thousand thoughts

the hole is inside us
it brims over
is empty and full at once.

Lillian Morrison

My Friend

Two days ago with dancing glancing hair,
   With living lips and eyes;
   Now pale, dumb, blind, she lies;
So pale, yet still so fair.

We have not left her yet, not yet alone;
   But soon must leave her where
   She will not miss our care,
Bone of our bone.

Weep not; O friends, we should not weep:
   Our friend of friends lies full of rest;
   No sorrow rankles in her breast,
Fallen fast asleep.

She sleeps below,
   She wakes and laughs above.
   To-day, as she walked, let us walk in love:
To-morrow follow so.

Christina Rossetti

An Old Story

Strange that I did not know him then,
  That friend of mine!
I did not even show him then
  One friendly sign;

But cursed him for the ways he had
  To make me see
My envy of the praise he had
  For praising me.

I would have rid the earth of him
  Once, in my pride . . .
I never knew the worth of him
  Until he died.

Edwin Arlington Robinson

On the Death of Friends
in Childhood

We shall not ever meet them bearded in heaven,
Nor sunning themselves among the bald of hell;
If anywhere, in the deserted schoolyard at twilight,
Forming a ring, perhaps, or joining hands
In games whose very names we have forgotten.
Come, memory, let us seek them there in the shadows.

Donald Justice

Remembrance

How many dear companions who enlivened for us
The world's rough road are gone, each fellow traveler
Much missed; yet say not sadly: they have left us!
But rather say, with gratitude: they were.

Vasily Zhukovsky

*translated from the Russian
by Babette Deutsch*

Like my cupped hands
Spilling drops back into the mountain pool
And clouding its pure waters
Before the satisfaction of my thirst,
So have I had to part from you too soon.

Tsurayuki

translated from the Japanese

John's Song

It's a long walk in the dark
on the blind side of the moon
and it's a long day without water
when the river's gone
and it's hard listening to no voice
when you're all alone

so take a hundred lighted candles with you
when you walk on the moon
and quickly quickly tie a knot in the river
before the water's gone
and listen for my voice, if for no other
when you're all alone

Joan Aiken

Index of Authors

Index of Titles

Index of First Lines

I saw many friends, and among them the friend I loved most 85
I saw you walking 11
I shot a golf ball into the air; 55
I want to write a poem 14
I went by footpath and by stile 98
I'd fill up the house with guests this minute 43
If I should die tonight 47
In autumn, chained to classrooms, we still can hear 30
It may have been the pride in me for aught 92
It's a long walk in the dark 105

Kyrnos, be flexible in character, always adapting 16

let it go—the 79
Like a quetzal plume, a fragrant flower, 22
Like my cupped hands 104

May God preserve you in the same way, 23
My friend attacks my friend 62

Oh, sure am I when come to die, 40
On St. Martin's evening green 32

Remember me when I am gone away, 93
River's glint and mountain mist were floating in green; 89

So long as we speak the same language and never understand each
    other, 46
Some of my best friends are white boys. 35
Something vague waxes or wanes. 76
Spring wine . . . autumn wine, give me 28
Strange that I did not know him then, 101
Strangest of gaps 99

That she forgot me was the least 80
The factory on the river, during lunch 91

113

Index of Translators